STORYTIME COLLECTION

Storytime

A TRELD BICKNELL BOOK

First published in Great Britain 1975 by The Bodley Head Ltd.
This revised edition first published 1993
in the United States of America by Whispering Coyote Press,
P.O. Box 2159, Halesite, New York 11743-2159.

Printed in Singapore for Imago Publishing

Library of Congress Cataloging-in-Publication Data

Roffey, Maureen
The grand old Duke of York/illustrated by Maureen Roffey; additional
verses by Bernard Lodge, —Rev. ed.
p.   cm.
"A Treld Bicknell book"—T.p. verso.
Summary: The grand old Duke of York marches his men up and down and all
around. In new verses, added to the original nursery rhyme, he gradually
loses all his men and then finds them again.
ISBN 1-879085-79-8
1. Nursery rhymes. 2. Children's poetry. [1. Nursery rhymes.]
I. Lodge, Bernard, II. Title.
PZ8.3.R63Gr-1993

398.8—dc20   92-21229   CIP   AC

The Grand Old Duke of York

Illustrated by Maureen Roffey
Additional verses by Bernard Lodge

Whispering Coyote Press, Inc./New York

The grand old Duke of York,
He had ten thousand men.
He marched them up to the top of the hill,
And he marched them down again.

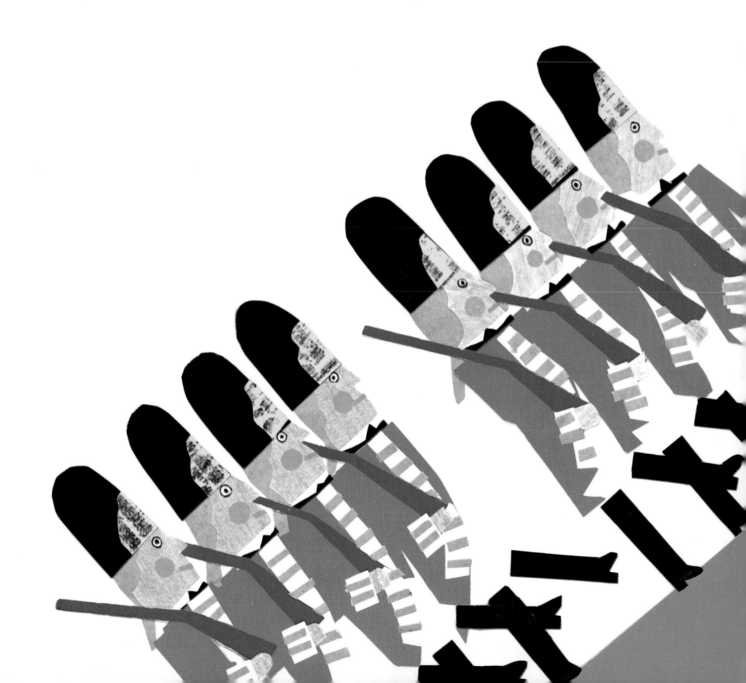

And when they were up, they were up,
And when they were down, they were down,
And when they were only half-way up,
They were neither up nor down.

The grand old Duke of York,
Then had five hundred men.
He marched them in and out of a wood,
And marched them in again.

And some turned to the left,
And some turned to the right,
And some marched all around the wood,
Till day turned into night.

The grand old Duke of York,
His men were half asleep.
He marched them through a river,
But the river was too deep.

And some of them did sink,
And some of them did swim,
And some did firmly shake his hand
And bid farewell to him.

The grand old Duke of York,
Had only twenty men—
Fifteen marching through a farm,
Were chased off by a hen.

And two were lost in a barn,
And two were lost in a sty,
And the only soldier who was left,
Ran off and waved goodbye

The grand old Duke of York,
He found himself alone.
He sat right down on top of a drum,
And there did weep and moan.

He threw away his sword,
He threw away his gun,
And then he wished that all his travels
Never had begun.

The grand old Duke of York,
He heard a bugle sound—
As he buckled on his sword and gun,
His heart began to pound.

He saw them in rows of five,
He saw them in rows of ten.
They all lined up in front of him
The Duke's ten thousand men.

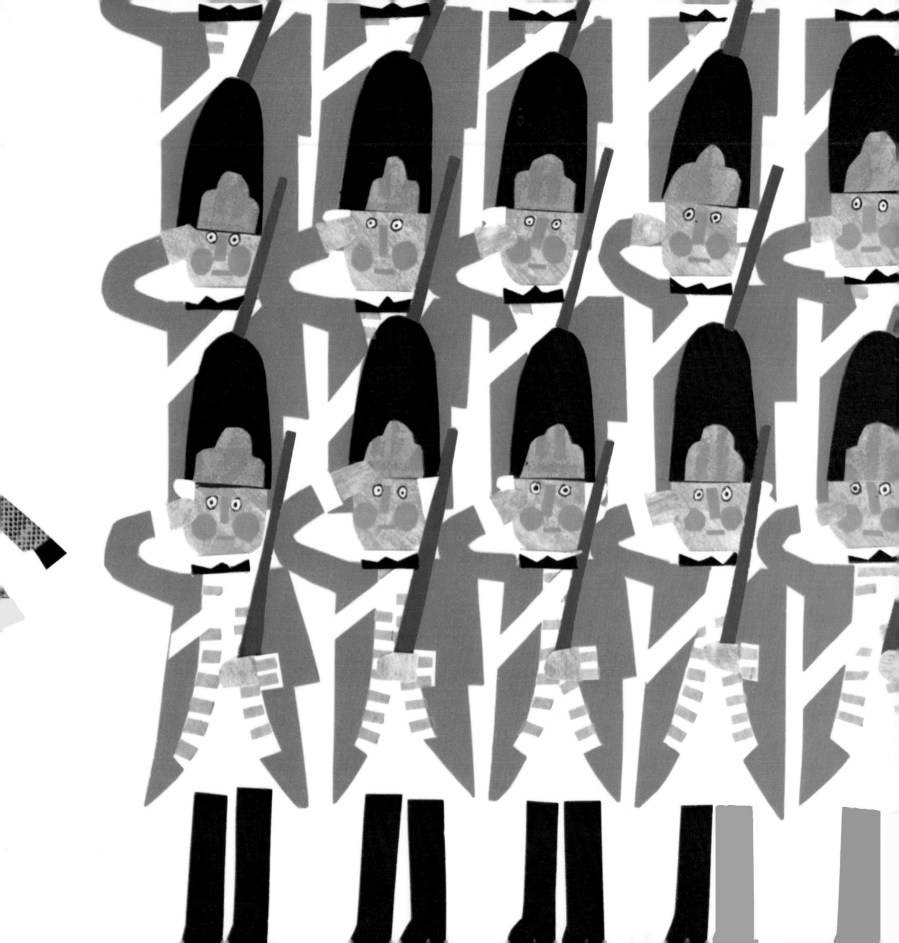

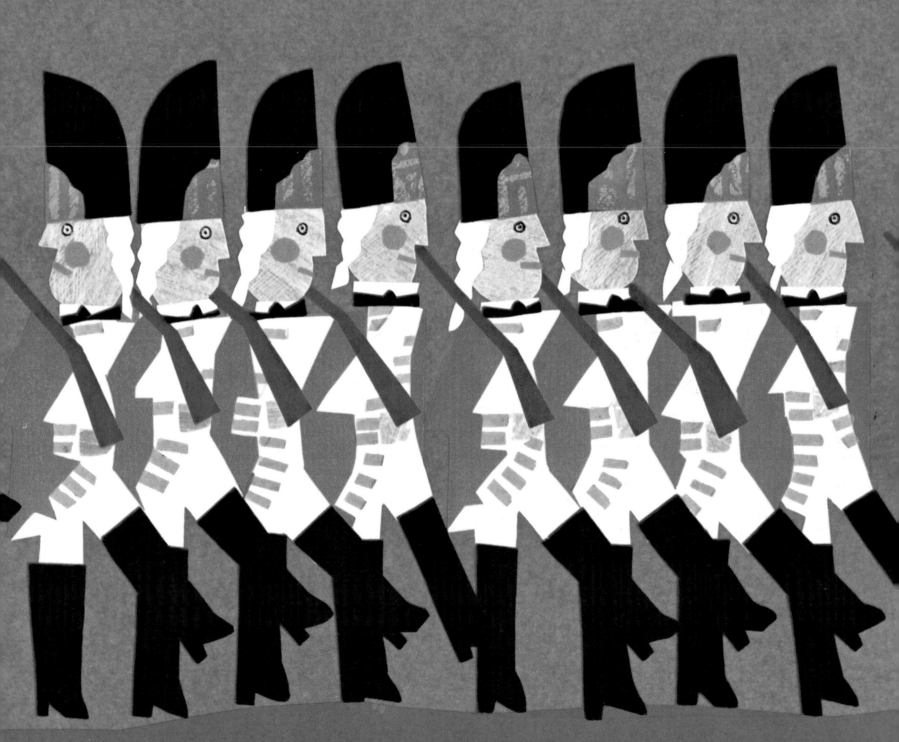